"The King's Kid"

By Karen "Lady Kay" Hilton-Sanders

This book is dedicated to

My Grandson Jasiah,

Grandson Omari that's resting easy in Heaven,

And

My Godchildren Layla and Jamir

Written by Karen "Lady Kay" Hilton-Sanders
Illustrated by R Van Hermawan

ISBN 9781686599255
Copyright December 2018

I AM the King's Kid

I AM the King's Kid
I have; I AM; and I will forever be

All that The King has created me to be

I AM
Unique in every way

I AM
grateful for The Kings Blessings that fill my day

The King watches over me
Both day and night

He is a lamp unto my feet

The King is my guiding light.

I AM never alone
Because the King is always near.

The King is my protector
So, I have nothing to fear.

The King guides my steps
Throughout my day.

And with HIS guidance
I know exactly what to say.

I AM the King's Kid

I was born to win

And I am never ever alone
Because the King lives within

And when it's time for me to rest
I just lay down my head

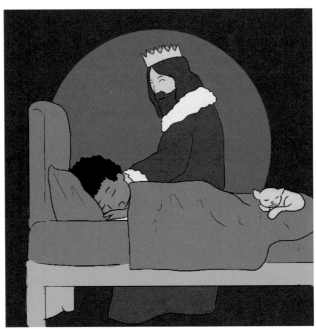

And while I dream the King watches over me
While I AM asleep in my bed.

I AM _____
and I Am the King's Kid

King's Kid Pledge

I, _____ am The King's Kid

I love God and I Love others

And I love myself too

I honor and obey my parents

I won't steal or lie

I won't hurt others or myself

I will live by what the Bible says

I will forever be The King's Kid

King's Kid Prayer

Before I lay down I just want to say
Thank you Lord for the beautiful day
Thank you for being my side
Thank you for your love
Thanks for watching over me from above
I made it this day because of you
Thank you for my mother, father and all of my family
Thank you for all of your help
Thank you for sweet dreams and good sleep
Thank you for always being here with me
In Jesus name Amen

"You were created by God to be someone special. Someone who would change the world and make it a better place for everyone."

- You are amazing
- You are powerful
- You are wonderful
- You are the KING'S Kid

Karen "Lady Kay" Hilton- Sanders

Jennifer & Xander,

Blessings to you both. Thanks for giving God glory out of your life.

Love

Wendy King

Made in the USA
Lexington, KY
04 December 2019

57919105R10017